THE SUPADUPA KID

written by
TY ALLAN JACKSON

illustrated by
JONATHAN SHEARS

Published by Big Head Books

© 2010 by Tyrone Allan Jackson

Library of Congress Control Number
2012912038

ISBN: 978-0-615-66598-6

Printed in the U.S.A.

WOR 19 5

This book is dedicated to my brother, Javon Jackson, for teaching me one of life's most powerful lessons;

Tomorrow is not promised.

And to my wife, Martique Jackson, for teaching me everything else.

The Supadupa Kid

By Ty Allan Jackson

1

My name is Javon Williams. I'm a twelve-year-old student at Booker T. Washington Elementary and Middle School in Littletown, New York. My hobbies are listening to music, playing baseball, and rescuing the city from peril. You see, my friends know me as the skinny kid with the big dimples. But for those who get bullied out of their lunch money or get wedgies so often that they carry extra underwear, I go by another name - The Supadupa Kid and this is my story.

The day started out like any other Monday morning. I was getting ready for school and Denise, my six-year-old sister was doing everything in her power to make us late. She's the nosiest kid in the world, and she sticks that nose into everything I do then reports it all to Mom.

Just yesterday I was sitting at the kitchen table eating a big bowl of Kooky Crunch cereal when I spilled the milk. It wasn't a lot of milk but as soon as the milk hit the table, Denise started screaming "Ooooh, I'm tellin' Mom." Of course, Mom said it was no big deal—but still, there was Denise, with her arms folded and that smug look on her face that drives me crazy. Was I going to cry over spilt milk? Nope! I just cleaned it up and got us on our way to school.

Some times, we take the bus to school, but most days we walk. Every day on our way to school, Denise bugs me. She yaps on and on, asking a million questions like why my room is so messy and how come she has to walk to school with her brother, and why couldn't she have a cute big sister instead of a bone-head like me. Man, that girl really drives me nuts. The only person who gets under my skin more than Denise is

Hoody. Hoody is the local bully who wears black hooded sweatshirts, even in the summertime! He terrorizes the entire neighborhood, and unfortunately, I'm his favorite target. He's twelve years old, just like me, but twice my size with half the brains and all the mean. Some kids on the block say he was raised by wolves and dropped off on his parent's doorstep because he kept giving the other wolves rabies. Hoody's parents think he's the sweetest kid in town. Little do they know the only sweet thing about Hoody is the desserts he steals from kids at lunchtime.

Every morning, on our way to school, Hoody does something to annoy me. Last Friday, he hit me in the head with a balloon filled with vinegar right before Mrs. Davies' first period math test. I had to sit in the back of the class smelling like a caesar salad until Mom brought me a change of clothes. This morning I knew Hoody would be up to something, but little did I know that his antics would change both of our lives forever.

The weather forecast for the day said it would be partly cloudy with a chance of afternoon thunderstorms, and since my dad is the local weatherman on channel WCRZ, he always makes sure Denise and I are prepared for whatever Mother Nature dishes out. So, we both had ponchos tucked in our backpacks and I had a super-sized umbrella for us to share, if it happened to rain. Despite Denise's constant complaining, the walk to school was going smoothly until out of nowhere Hoody snatched my umbrella and ran off with it. I took off after him and left Denise standing there shaking her head. He rounded a corner and I lost track of him for a moment. When I caught up to him, I saw him jumping out from behind a tree and running away without my umbrella. I knew he did something to it so I approached the tree carefully. There it was. The umbrella looked perfectly fine. I didn't see any boogers or hamster poop on it so I figured Hoody was just being his normal jerky self and wanted to make me late for school. I picked up my umbrella, shrugged my shoulders, caught up with Denise and got us to school on time, not giving the umbrella a second thought.

2

For a Monday, school was the bomb. I got an A on Mrs. Davies' math test. We had pizza for lunch, and Erika Harris, the cutest girl in school actually spoke to me. Erika is the number one "IT" girl in the whole school. She isn't just the prettiest girl in school, she's smart too. She's captain of the debate team and the starting point guard on the girls' basketball team. Her mom is the chief physician at the local hospital and her dad is one of those hot shot lawyers you see on TV with the crazy phone number like 1-800-sue-them-all or something like that. Not to mention her brother is the quarterback of the high school football team. The Harris family has it going on, so having Erika say hi to me, was pretty much like hitting the lottery on my birthday while on vacation in Hawaii. What made life even better was that I hadn't bumped into Hoody since the umbrella incident.

After school, I met up with Denise and couldn't stop thinking about what a great day I was having. We were halfway home when it started to rain. I let Denise put on her poncho first because I didn't want to huddle under the umbrella with her until it was absolutely necessary. Then the rain really started to come down in buckets. As I pulled out the umbrella, I noticed Erika on the corner getting soaked. I couldn't believe my luck, here was my chance to play the hero. I took a deep breath, walked over to her and offered her my umbrella. She took it and gave me a smile that made my ears tingle. Her smile soon faded when she couldn't open it. She handed it back to me but I couldn't get it open either. All of a sudden Hoody shows up.

"Give it to me wimp, I'll open it for you," he said as he snatched the umbrella out of my hands.

"I got it, Hoody!" I shouted and snatched it back. Next thing you knew we were in a tug-of-war fighting for control of the umbrella. We were yanking and pulling so hard that neither of us noticed that we had knocked Erika and Denise down. We had our hands on the umbrella handle when it finally opened. Something slimy and sticky oozed down onto our hands. It was so sticky that I couldn't let it go and neither could Hoody.

There was a strange odor too, like how the air smells after a fireworks show. I felt goose bumps all over and the hair on my arms stood up. That's when it happened. Suddenly, there was a tremendous **KA-BOOM** and a huge bolt of lightning blasted out of the sky and zapped the umbrella. A dark cloud of smoke covered us as the ground trembled. A painful jolt shot through my body and then everything went black.

3

When I opened my eyes everything was white. White walls, white floors—I was even wearing white pajamas. I figured I was in heaven until I heard Denise's big mouth. Then I thought I might be in H.E. double hockey sticks. Then I heard my Mom and Dad, and I knew I was in the hospital. Mom was crying and Dad was standing above me with a look on his face I will never forget.

"How are you feeling, son?" he asked.

I was a little weak and my hands and feet felt numb, but I was okay.

"It's a true miracle that you are in one piece. Who would think a skinny kid like you could take a blast from a lightning bolt? You're much sturdier than you look and you're lucky to be alive." Dr. Harris said as she shone a light in my eyes.

They told me about the lightning that hit the umbrella. The doctor also told me that the glue on the umbrella handle may have saved my life.

"Glue, what glue?" I asked confused.

"Your friend put glue on your umbrella as a prank," Dr. Harris said.

So that's what Hoody was doing behind the tree. He was putting glue on the inside of the umbrella, so it could drop on my head when I opened it. The creep! So why did he try to take it from me if he knew the glue was in it? That dude is even dumber than he looks.

"Hey, Doc, what happened to Hoody?"

"He left the hospital four days ago."

"FOUR DAYS AGO! How long have I been in here?"

"You've been in a coma for two weeks," Mom said.

"Wow, I've been knocked out for two weeks! My breath must be really funky!"

4

Three days after I left the hospital, I was feeling pretty good. I was dying to go back to school, but my parents thought I needed to relax for a few more days—although having Denise bugging me most of the time hadn't been exactly relaxing.

It was on the fourth day that I began to notice some strange things happening around the house. One afternoon I woke up after a nap to find that my computer, my game system and every light in my room had been turned on. That stuff wasn't on when I went to sleep. Denise was at school so she couldn't have done it, and Mom had no idea either. I also noticed that whenever I passed the TV the picture would get all fuzzy. The weirdest thing of all was when I picked up a bag of microwave popcorn, and it started popping before I even put it in the microwave. That's when I started to worry. I couldn't tell Mom I was a walking microwave because she would just overreact, and if I told my Dad he would probably send me to NASA to be examined. There was no way I was going to tell my big mouth sister because the last secret I told her got me grounded for a month. So I called Ronald. He's been my best friend since we were babies. He's more like a brother than a friend, although no one would ever confuse us for brothers. I'm real skinny, and he's a little pudgy. Whenever we stand next to each other, kids say we look like the number ten.

Ronald is super smart. He's a straight A student in every class and his favorite subject is science. He's won first prize at the state science fair three years in a row. You know the science experiment where you hook up a battery to a light bulb to make it glow? Well, Ronald figured out how to store his own electricity by using only a Styrofoam cup, a metal pan, a nail, and a battery. You could even see the sparks coming out of the cup. It was pretty cool. If anyone could help me figure this mess out it would be Ronald, so I was really happy when he came into my room. As we greeted each other with our usual secret handshake a spark shot from my fingers to his, startling us both.

"Ow, what in the name of Benjamin Franklin was that?" Ronald yelped.

"Whoa, dude? Are you ok, man?"

"My hand feels like it's on fire!" Ronald said blowing on his fingertips.

"Yo, this is why I called you. Something strange is happening to me. It was the lighting strike, I know it. It's affecting me somehow. Stuff has been freakin out on me. I blew up my toaster, shorted out the fridge and set my electric toothbrush on fire."

"Impossible! This is seriously strange."

"I'm not kidding, Ronald."

"I believe you, it just sounds so bizarre. Are you feeling any different?"

"I feel great! I feel fantastic actually!"

"No dizziness, fainting, or confusion?"

"Nope, I'm all good."

"Well then maybe we should perform a few experiments to enable us to fully understand what's going on with you."

"Okay, but I'm not wearing those gowns where my buns are hanging out again!"

Ronald took the light bulb out of my lamp.

"Here, take this, see if you can make it glow," he said.

I looked at Ronald like he was crazy. I couldn't make it glow, could I? My heart started to pound. What if I could make it glow? What would that mean? Could I be turning into some kind of human generator? I closed my eyes and grabbed the bulb and...nothing happened.

"Phew!" *That was a relief*, I thought to myself as I tried to give the bulb back.

"Wait a moment; the experiment is not quite complete. Concentrate on something exciting, let's get your adrenaline pumping before you give me the bulb back. Perhaps it's an emotional stimulus that triggers the phenomenon."

"What?" I asked.

"When you're excited, electrons pump through the grey matter in your brain and stimulate the body. I hypothesize that such stimulation could create a reaction that may illuminate the light bulb."

"I'm sorry, Ronald, I don't speak geek."

"Just do it!"

"Do what?"

"GET HAPPY!"

"Oh. Why didn't you say that in the first place? Okay, I'll give it a try." I thought about hitting a home run in the ninth inning to win the World Series, and then I could feel energy coursing through my body. My hands began to tingle and then the bulb started to glow. Dim at first, then brighter, and brighter, and brighter until **POP!** The light bulb shattered into a million pieces. Ronald and I just looked at each other in silence. Then suddenly his eyes grew bigger, and he stumbled backwards until his back hit the wall. He was scaring the heck out of me.

"Wha...what's wrong?" I stammered. I looked down and

realized that I was hovering six inches off the floor.

5

That night I couldn't sleep a wink. I was afraid that if I started to dream and got too excited I might light the bed on fire. I wasn't tired though. I felt energized, I felt pumped and I felt, well, charged up! I decided to go outside in the backyard. It was one o'clock in the morning, and all the neighboring houses were dark. The cool night air really made me feel good. I walked on the grass and tried to think of good thoughts. I wondered if I could release some of the energy from my body like I did with the light bulb. I did what Ronald told me to do, and I thought about Erika. Immediately I felt a tingle in my hands and my fingertips started to glow and then **ZAP**!

A bolt of electricity shot through my fingertips down to the ground and blasted a hole in the lawn. *Dad's not going to be happy about this*. I was scared and excited at the same time, but I had to try it again. I thought about riding a rollercoaster and **ZAP!** It happened again. I tried to control the intensity of the bolt and make it stronger. I thought about Grandma's sweet potato pie and **BOOM!!!!**

Whoa, I could get used to this. It was getting a little easier every time, and I was getting happier by the minute. I could feel the energy pumping through my body. The glow of my fingertips reminded me of the sparklers I love to light on the Fourth of July. I was getting the hang of shooting energy bolts but I really wanted to know how I managed to float six inches off the ground. I tried to concentrate. I thought of scoring a touchdown, watching an action movie, even going to see my favorite rapper in concert, but nothing. I couldn't get off the ground. I was getting a little tired and decided to try again tomorrow when I heard the most terrifying sound in the world.

"Oooooooh, I'm telling Mom!" It was Denise. "What are you doing outside this time of night and why did you put all those holes in the ground? Did you hide one of my dolls in those holes? What are you looking for? Are you looking for buried treasure? What was all that noise?"

"Denise, Denise, shh. Keep your voice down, you're gonna wake up Mom and Dad!" I whispered.

"I don't care!" she said.

"If you be quiet, I'll do your chores for a week."

"This is worth at least a month of chores," Denise demanded.

"Deal!" I said, as I ran back into the house.

6

Usually on Saturday mornings I've got a big bowl of cereal and cartoons on lockdown, but not today. I convinced my parents I was well enough to go outside and hang out with Ronald. I had to show him what I could do. Maybe he could give me some ideas on getting this floating off the ground. We went to the school baseball field and crept behind the bleachers where I showed him my new lightning bolt trick. After seeing a few of these, Ronald went crazy.

"In the name of Isaac Newton, this is the greatest thing in the history of mankind! Have you told your parents yet?"

"No way. I don't want you breathing a word of this to anyone. This is our secret. We can do great things with this power. I've just got to learn to control it." I said.

Ronald giggled, "Yeah, you've got the power all right, the power to cook your food without using a microwave."

"How did you know that, I didn't even tell you about the popcorn," I said but Ronald ignored me.

"By the way, what do you mean *we* can do great things?" Ronald asked suspiciously.

"Come on Ron, you're a scientific genius. Only you can help me put this power to good use."

"Good use? I'm not certain I like the sound of that. What do you think you're going to do, save the world?"

"Maybe?" I said with a sly smirk on my face. Ronald's eyes lit up like he'd just gotten a new microscope for Christmas.

"WOW, theoretically, that could actually work! We could make you into a real live superhero, not just some movie or comic book weirdo in tight pajamas flying around saving pretty girls. You could be the real thing. I'm with you, partner!" he said giving me a high five as I accidently zapped him. "OUCH!" he moaned.

"Oops."

"You really have to learn to control that! Jeepers, my best friend has turned into a human bug zapper," Ronald said as he blew on his fingertips. "In order for us to determine how to control these amazing attributes we must start from the beginning. Come on."

"Where are we going?" I asked as I grabbed my jacket.

"I told you, we're going to the beginning. To the very location where you and Hoody where hit by that lightning bolt."

"What's this?" Ronald asked as we approached the tree where Hoody sabotaged the umbrella. He put on a pair of rubber gloves and pulled a pair of tweezers and a plastic baggie out of his shirt pocket. Using the tweezers he picked up an empty tube of glue and dropped it in the baggie before reading the label carefully.

"Supadupa Glue, very interesting," Ronald said.

"What's so interesting about an empty tube of glue?" I asked.

"The ingredients in the glue are unlike anything I've ever seen before. The glue is manufactured by a company called Microtech. I can't determine its chemical composition here but maybe somehow the elements in the glue fused with the energy from the lightning. Then the electricity must have somehow altered your molecules and biogenetic structure, giving you these special powers. But that is simply a hypothesis. I'd have to run some tests to make sure my theory is correct," Ronald said.

"I didn't understand a word you said, but thanks for the explanation, Einstein. Let's just take the tube back to your house. I feel like we're being watched."

7

When we got to Ronald's house we put the tube of Supadupa Glue away and focused on flying. Thanks to the light bulb test, we knew I could float, and so I could probably fly. We just had to figure out how. Ronald had a big back yard that was surrounded by a high brick wall, so we didn't have to worry about nosy neighbors. Ronald's parents weren't home from work yet and his big sister, Wanda, was too busy talking on the phone to pay any attention to us. First, I tried to focus on good thoughts, but that only created the lightning bolts. I popped a few into Ronald's lawn just for the fun of it, but my feet never left the ground.

"What were you doing when you floated the first time?" Ronald asked.

I thought for a moment, scratching my head, "I was holding a light bulb?"

"In the name of Thomas Edison, that's it! You were holding a light bulb!" he shouted, then ran into his house and brought back a light bulb. He handed it to me, and I looked at it, confused.

"Go ahead, light it up!" he said.

I held it in my hand and thought of mom's chocolate chip cookies, and instantly my body felt lighter and then—WOW, I was floating. The better the thought, the higher I got. I got about four feet off the ground when I dropped the bulb. When the bulb fell, so did I.

"How am I doing this?" I asked while rubbing my sore butt.

"I'm not sure but I doubt it's the glass, it's most definitely not the filament. Perhaps it's not the bulb itself but the metal in the base of the bulb. Somehow that metal must help you fly, but we'll have to do more experiments to confirm.

"Sweet, but I can't hold a light bulb all the time—that would cramp my style."

"It's a safe assumption that as long as you have something metal on, like a belt or watch, you should be able to fly, although it could depend on the type of metal used. It could be nickel, platinum, silver— maybe even something simple like aluminum."

"Okay, you're losing me again."

"I believe the base of a light bulb is made of either steel or aluminum. I'll be right back!" Ronald ran into the house again and brought out a silver ball.

"What's that?" I asked.

"A ball of aluminum foil. I got it from the kitchen. Try it." I took it and ZOOM! I flew about ten feet into the air so fast I thought I was gonna hurl.

"Get me down!" I screamed.

"Holy Wilbur Wright!" Ronald yelled as he ran around the yard with his arms spread wide preparing to catch me.

"Ronald, get me down!"

"Ease up your grip on the foil." He suggested. When I did I slowly floated to the ground. When I gripped it tighter, I shot back up into the sky.

"Ronald, you're a genius." I soared over his head. That's when Wanda opened up her bedroom window.

"What are you losers doing?" she demanded. Fortunately, I was close enough to a tree so I grabbed onto the branches and pretended I was climbing it.

"Nothing, just hanging around," I said. She shook her head and went back inside.

"Phew, that was close."

"It sure was!" Ronald said, gasping for breath. "Come on inside, I'm thirsty. I'll make us some chocolate milk, but don't blame me if yours ends up being hot cocoa."

8

I woke up the next morning to the smell of smoke. I looked around my bed relieved that it wasn't on fire. I went to the kitchen to see if mom was cooking something.

"Hey, Mom, is there something burning?"

"No, Javon. There must be a fire somewhere. I heard fire trucks go by a little while ago."

"Cool, can I go check it out?" I was determined to find out where the fire was coming from.

"Of course not, fires are dangerous. Besides, you haven't had your breakfast, and you didn't brush your teeth yet, yuck mouth! Besides, I have some errands to run today and I'll need your help".

As we got into the car I noticed smoke rising in the air only a few blocks away. The fire was closer than I thought. As we drove to the store I saw that Daisy Street was blocked off. There were fire trucks, police cars, and ambulances all over the place. I wished I could help but who was I kidding, I'm no hero.

Traffic was at a standstill as people stopped and stared. Then it hit me! I knew that house. That was Hoody's house. The house was completely destroyed. Firefighters were still putting out the last smoldering embers. Police officers were walking around asking questions.

Oh no! I really hadn't given Hoody a lot of thought since I got home from the hospital. I completely forgot that he got struck by lightning too. What if Hoody is going through the same thing I'm going through? What if he has the same powers I do but can't control them either and set his own house on fire?

I noticed Hoody's parents talking to a police officer. His mom was crying. As the officer walked away, I saw a kid with his back turned to me. It had to be Hoody because even though it was 90 degrees outside, he was wearing the same thing he usually wears—black boots, black jeans, and a black hooded sweatshirt. He turned around and looked at me as if he knew I was staring at him. He had an evil grin on his face that gave me the creeps. His smile widened then he pulled his sunglasses down just enough for me to see his eyes. His eyes, black at first, gradually got brighter. In a matter of seconds they changed from black to yellow to bright red before turning back to black again. I couldn't believe what I had just seen.

"Mom, did you see that?"

"See what?" she asked.

"Hoody's eyes, did you see his eyes?

"No honey. What's wrong with his eyes?"

"Nothing, it was nothing," I said but at the same time I was thinking to myself, *Oh, it was something, a really big something*!

9

Later that afternoon, Ronald asked me to come over to his house. He said he had a surprise for me. I rang the doorbell, and Wanda opened the door. As usual, her head was connected to her cell phone. She simply pointed upstairs and walked away. I found Ronald in his room, smiling from ear to ear, and holding a box.

"What's in the box? I asked.

"You're in the box," he said, still grinning.

"What are you talking about?

"Here, see for yourself." I opened the box and saw what looked like orange pajamas and a pair of boots.

"What the heck is this?"

"It's your suit," he said.

"My what?"

"Your suit! I got it online. It's made of durable fabric that's heat resistant and the boots have steel toes. The metal inside the boots should help you fly. I got it in orange, your favorite color and I designed the lightning bolt across the chest. It's perfect! So what do you think?" I was speechless. Not because the suit was awesome but because I couldn't believe this was really happening. Was I really going to try being a superhero? Could I really do this? I'm just a kid.

Ronald could see the fear on my face. He looked me in the eye and put his hand on my shoulder.

"Javon, these powers you've been given are a gift. There is a reason this gift was given to you. They should be used to help people, to make a difference. Now try the suit on and let's go save the world."

"Man that was corny—inspiring, but corny. Okay, fine. I'll put the suit on."

It fit perfectly. I felt like a different person. I knew from that moment on, life would never be the same for me.

"Alright, Ronald, let's go save the world!"

"Wait, there's one last thing."

"Now what?"

"We have to hide your identity. All superheroes do it. Besides, our parents would ground us for life if they knew what we were up to." Ronald said nervously.

"I can hear my mom now, *'Javon Williams, get your butt outta the sky and put some clothes on!'* With a mask on she could only say,

'What mother would allow her child to fly around the city in his long underwear.' You're right Ronald, I need a mask".

"Well, you're lucky I'm a genius because I bought one of those too!" Ronald said pulling a mask out of the box.

"Okay, I've got the suit; I've got the mask and the boots. I'm ready to go. Now, where am I going?"

"I'm glad you asked. Check this out." Ronald said holding up something small.

"What is it?"

"I call it a Ron-Com. I've got one too. It's a communication device that I designed so we can talk with one another.

"This is awesome Ronald!"

"Oh, but there's more! I can go online and get emergency information from our local police emergency database and even get their 911 calls."

"You can do that? My best friend is a twelve year old hacker!" I interrupted.

"Shhh…" Ronald said nervously. "I'm no hacker. It's perfectly legal. I'm a member of the New York Scanner Club. It's a hobby."

"Ronald, you're a weird dude, but I'm glad you're on my side."

"When I hear a 911 call I think you can handle, I will relay the information to you, and you can fly to the location and you know...kick butt, beat the bad guys, save the day!"

"Save the day, huh?" I asked, and we both burst out laughing. I was as ready as I could be when Ronald gave me my first assignment.

"There is a cat stuck up a tree at 105 Linden Street. This is perfect!"

"Are you kidding? You want me to fly to Linden Street to rescue a cat?"

"You can't possibly mess this up. Besides, it's your first call; we should start out small," Ronald said. I shrugged my shoulders, opened his window, and jumped out.

"Away I go!" I shouted as I zipped into the sky. Although it was my first real flight, it seemed pretty easy. It felt kind of like riding a bike in the sky. As long as I kept a look out for birds, trees, and telephone wires, I was all good. Linden Street was just a few blocks away so I got there quickly. As I flew over the house I could see a white, fluffy cat stuck in a tree. There was a little girl with red pigtails begging the cat to come down. When she saw me flying in, her eyes got as big as saucers. I came in for a not so smooth landing and skidded on my butt. *Note to self, practice landing.*

"You were flying! How were you doing that?" she gasped.

"I eat lots of vegetables. Is that your cat?"

"Yeah, that's my cat, are those your tights?" She giggled.

"They're not tights." I snapped, before flying up to the cat. The cat looked surprised to see me. I gently grabbed the fur ball and started down but I was so excited that I accidently gave the cat a little **ZAP.** It hissed and leaped out of my arms.

Thankfully the little girl was there to catch it.

"Oh Fluffy, you're safe now." The little girl cooed. The cat looked at me and hissed again. Its white fur was now standing straight up, and scorched with brown and black patches. There was also smoke coming from its tail.

"Look what you did to Fluffy!"

"But..but...at least I got it out of the tree." I said, but the little girl looked at me angrily.

"What's your name?" she demanded.

"My name?" I repeated. Ronald and I hadn't thought about a name but suddenly it came to me. *The name of the glue that gave me these powers, that's what I'll call myself.* "I'm The Supadupa Kid!" I said in as deep a voice as I could.

"Well, I'm telling my daddy that some scoopa-poopa kid toasted my kitty cat." She kicked me in the shin and ran into the house screaming for her mom and dad.

Uh oh, time for me to get outta here. I flew back to Ronald's house and told him what happened. We both laughed so hard that he got a headache, and I accidently zapped a hole in his carpet. He decided it might be a good idea to keep a fire extinguisher near me whenever I was in the house. I agreed.

10

Monday morning arrived, and I was finally going back to school. It was the usual morning routine— getting dressed for school, eating a big bowl of Kooky Crunch cereal, and Denise getting on my nerves. But I have to admit that I felt different. I was excited that I was going back with an incredible secret, a secret that only Ronald and I knew about. Well, maybe. What made me nervous was that there might be another person who had the same secret— Hoody. If Hoody and I had the same powers, how would I be able to stop him? Would we eventually come to a showdown, a fight to the finish? But maybe Hoody doesn't have the same powers. Maybe the glow of his eyes was just the glare of the sun. Yeah, that's it. I bet it was just my imagination.

As I was walking with Denise to school I bumped into Erika. She asked me how I was feeling and what it felt like to be struck by lightning. Boy, if I could only tell her the truth. She said I've been the talk of the school and everyone was excited that I was coming back. When I finally walked into the classroom, all my classmates mobbed me. They gave me hugs and pats on the back. They asked me all kinds of questions like, how did it feel? Did it hurt? Can I glow in the dark? It was pretty cool being the center of attention. The teacher, Mr. McMillan, asked me to stand in front of the class and tell my story. So I did. I told the class everything about the incident—from the glue on the umbrella to what kind of ice cream the nurses gave me at the hospital. Of course, I left out a few details.

Throughout my story I would give a wink to Ronald, who was sitting in the back of the classroom.

He just smiled and winked back. As I was wrapping up there was a loud ringing in the hallways. It was the fire alarm. Principal Dean's voice came over the loud speaker. *"THIS IS NOT A DRILL, THIS IS NOT A DRILL. TEACHERS, PLEASE ESCORT THE STUDENTS OUT OF THE BUILDING IN AN ORDERLY MANNER. I REPEAT THIS IS NOT A DRILL."* I followed my teacher out of the room and quickly caught up to Ronald, "Are you thinking what I'm thinking?"

"Hoody!" we both said at the same time. We scanned the crowd for Hoody but didn't see him anywhere. I knew he was somehow responsible for this, but he was nowhere to be found.

"Cindy, is Hoody here today?" I asked a girl from his class.

"Yes. He went to the restroom and while he was out the fire alarm went off. He's probably still in there." She said and hurried along with the rest of the students.

"I've gotta find him," I whispered to Ronald.

"Okay, I'll cover for you as long as I can. Just hurry, and be careful!"

I nodded and ducked into the crowd, heading as fast as I could towards the boy's bathroom down the hall. I managed to get by Mr.

McMillan without him noticing. I slipped silently into the bathroom and was surprised to find it empty. No Hoody. No anybody. I was headed for the door when I noticed that the window was open. It's always closed, so I walked over slowly and looked out. There he was, standing right under the flagpole in front of the building. It was like he was waiting for me to find him. In case of an emergency, that's where all the students and faculty are supposed to meet. He was the only one standing there, and he had his arms crossed. He didn't move a muscle and he still had his sunglasses on. I was hoping he would show me the color of his eyes, just to confirm what I thought I saw, but no luck. Instead, he just stood there motionless. He completely ignored me and it was ticking me off.

"Hoody, stay right there, we need to talk!" I yelled out the window. Just then the bathroom door opened. I turned to find a teacher in the doorway.

"Young man, you can't be in here. You need to leave now!"

"Yes, sir, I'm going." I said and took another quick look out the window but Hoody was gone. *Where did he go? How did he disappear so quickly?* I could now see the kids and teachers rushing from the school and heading towards the flagpole. There was no sign of Hoody. I lost him. I could hear sirens approaching the school and the smell of smoke started to fill the building. I left with the teacher and joined my classmates outside.

Yellow school buses showed up immediately to take us to Rosa Parks High School. I caught up with Ronald and asked him if he had seen Hoody but he hadn't. He did overhear the firefighters discussing the fire. They said the fire started in the basement in the maintenance room. The good thing was that the fire hadn't spread any further. The firefighters thought that the incident could have started with an electrical fire, but were not so sure. They couldn't seem to figure out what could have started it.

"I know it was Hoody. We've got to find him and get to the bottom of this. Hopefully, he's on one of these buses, and we can confront him."

"WE?" Ronald shouted. "Let's get this straight. I'm the brains of the operation, and you're the muscle. I am not trying to end up like a burnt piece of bacon. No thanks. You're on your own this time!"

11

Once we arrived at the high school, all the students were sent to the auditorium. Our principal, Mr. Dean, announced that the fire had been contained, but due to police investigation the school would be closed for the week. All the students cheered and applauded. Then Principal Dean stated that although the school was closed, classes would still continue here at Rosa Parks High School. All the applause turned to boos.

"For the rest of the day you will all stay here in the auditorium. You'll watch a movie for the remainder of the morning, eat lunch and then be bused home. Your parents have been notified."

Ronald and I had no time for movies. We used the time to get a plan together. We had to figure out how to find and stop Hoody before things got really ugly.

After school I went home to let Mom know that I was okay and then headed straight to Ronald's house. Mom had told me that Hoody and his parents were staying with family on the west side of town, which was a quick bike ride away. Our plan was simple. Find Hoody and see what's up. We hopped on our bikes, put on our helmets, and took off.

Riding my bike isn't usually a problem but Ronald was making it hard for me. Every time we came to a red light or stop sign, he'd do something to crack me up. He would make a funny face or tell a "Ronald Joke", a joke so not funny it was hysterical. This is one of my favorites. What is the one animal you don't want to play cards with? A cheetah, get it? A CHEAT-ER. See what I mean, so terrible its funny! Sure, who doesn't like to laugh, but now with my new Supadupa powers, whenever I laughed the bike would float off the concrete a few inches. I told him to cut it out, someone was going to see us. But he didn't care. At one corner he made a face so goofy, I actually did a somersault on the bike. Wouldn't you know it, Officer Taylor drives by and gave us a look that wiped the smiles right off our faces.

When we finally turned the corner onto Hoody's grandmother's street we stopped dead in our tracks. Hoody was standing outside her house with his arms folded, sunglasses on, with that evil smirk on his face. I could tell that Ronald was scared to approach him, but I wasn't. We hopped off our bikes and walked over to him.

"Hey, Hoody, what's up?" I asked.

"Wow, wasn't that crazy, the fire at school today?" Ronald asked nervously. We all stood there for a moment, in an uncomfortable silence, then Hoody finally spoke.

"How does it feel?" Hoody growled.

"How does what feel?" I asked.

"Don't play dumb with me. The power, how does it feel? I know you have it just like I do. I can feel the energy flowing through you."

"Errrr...I think I'll just step back a few feet. I feel like I'm standing between two talking microwaves. My hair is starting to stand up on my head," Ronald said.

"BE QUIET, DORK!" Hoody yelled. Then he pulled down his glasses. His eyes started to glow a bright red, and suddenly a beam of red light shot out and hit Ronald in the stomach.

"OWWWW!" Ronald howled as he clutched his belly.

"Hey!" I shouted. "You can't do that to my friend!"

"I can do that and more, but it's nothing like what I'm going to do to you." Hoody's blood red eyes were now aiming at me. Just as he was ready to strike, his grandmother poked her head out the window.

"What's with all the racket out there?"

"Oh nothing Nana, we're just playing around." Hoody said in the sweetest voice.

"Well, keep it down. I'm trying to watch my game show."

"Okay, Nana."

"*NANA?!*" Ronald and I snickered.

"You idiots better stay out of my way. If I can light a school and my house on fire, just imagine what I can do to you, or your house, or your families!" He said before walking away.

"Are you okay, buddy?" I asked Ronald once Hoody was out of sight.

"Yeah, but now I know what a hot pocket feels like."

"Well, that proves it. Not only do we have the same powers, but that whacko is really setting stuff on fire."

"How are you going to stop him?" Ronald asked.

"I don't know. You're the brains of this operation, figure it out. In the meantime, let's get you home."

"That's a good idea. Maybe if I eat my stomach will stop hurting," said Ronald.

"Yeah, I am kinda hungry. For some reason I've got a craving for a hot pocket."

"Very funny," Ronald said.

12

The next few days at Rosa Parks High School flew by. All our classes were held either in the cafeteria, gym or the auditorium. I actually saw a lot of Hoody, but we barely looked at each other.

School days were pretty uneventful. The real adventures came after school when we met up at Ronald's house. After finishing our homework we listened to the 911 calls on the scanner, looking for a mission that I could take on that wasn't too dangerous and didn't involve rescuing kitty-cats from trees. Anything involving life and death situations were a no-no.

Then one afternoon there was an emergency call about a robbery at the Dollar Bill Bank on Main Street.

Ronald and I turned on the TV to watch it on the local news. The story was on nearly every channel. There were dozens of police cars and reporters in front of the bank. It looked like a scene right out of the movies. Ronald and I were glued to the TV.

'*This is Jimmy Hall reporting from Big City News, broadcasting live, here at the Dollar Bill Bank* where a vicious standoff is occurring between the Littletown Police Department and a group of bank robbers. So far, it appears that no one has been hurt, but the situation seems to be escalating rapidly. Officer Taylor is currently negotiating with the leader of this band of thugs. So far the robbers have insisted that their demands be met, claiming that if they aren't, the hostages will not get out alive.

"Ronald, I have to go in!"

"WHAT? No, this is far too dangerous."

"We just can't stand here and let innocent people get hurt. Not when we can do something about it."

"And what exactly are we going to do about it?" Ronald asked a little sarcastically.

"I don't know, but I have to do something," I said. Suddenly, Ronald looked a little sheepish.

"Just be careful," he said. "I don't want any holes in that suit. It wasn't cheap you know."

"I don't want any holes in the suit either...or me!" I responded.

"And you'd better take these," he said, handing me two tiny devices.

"Ronald, what in the world are these?"

"They're my new Ron-Coms. The previous ones were prototypes. These new babies have two-way, voice-activated speech amplifiers with noise reducers and ultra-sound microphones. Insert them in your ears, and we will be able to communicate as if we were standing right next to each other."

"Are you serious? You made these?" I asked amazed.

"Yup. I also took the liberty of placing a tiny tracking device in the lightning bolt of your suit so I will know your location at all times. You know, just in case you're kidnapped by an evil villain and held captive in his secret island lair, I will know where you are! I'm not saying I'll come and rescue you, but I'll know where you are. I've been working on these for years."

"Ronald, I've always wondered what you were doing while I was playing baseball. You're the man!"

"And don't you forget it!" Ronald said proudly. "Now get outta here and be careful."

"Don't worry. I'll be back in a supadupa minute."

As I flew across the sky, I started to wonder if I had gotten in over my head. Getting cats out of trees is one thing, stopping criminals from robbing a bank is another.

Over the past few weeks I had gotten really good at flying. I snuck out of the house nearly every night to practice speed control, take-offs, landings, turns, twist, and dives. I had never been identified flying but there did seem to be a lot more calls about giant orange birds flying around the city. Thankfully none of the calls were taken seriously.

Now, here I was on my way to the bank, praying that nobody would spot me. As I approached the scene of the crime I was feeling a little nervous. I couldn't believe how many people were there.

Police and fire fighters, paramedics, news crews, on-lookers—there were hundreds of people surrounding the bank. I wanted to land on the roof but the S.W.A.T. team had it on lock. I saw one of them point at me, but before the others could see me I flew into an open window on the second floor. It was a utility closet. Perfect.

"Ronald, I'm in the building," I shouted.

"There is no need to shout, Javon. I can hear you perfectly, even if you whisper. By the way, you need to be a little more careful with your flying. There was a report of an unidentified flying object, and one of the news crews caught you on tape. Luckily you were moving too fast for them to get a good shot of you. Try to stay undercover from now on."

"Oh no! I hope Mom and Dad aren't watching the news right now, but I can't be concerned about that. I've got a crime to foil!"

"Man, that was corny. You've got to work on your catch phrases."

I opened the door and cautiously looked into the hallway. A bad guy carrying the biggest gun I'd ever seen was just a few feet away and I could hear others yelling on the floor below me.

My heart started pounding when he looked in my direction. I closed the door and stepped back, and banged into a shelf, knocking over a few bottles.

"What was that?" Ronald yelled in my ear as the doorknob began to turn.

"There's a guy with a gun right outside the door, and he knows I'm here," I whispered. Just as I feared: bad guy number one pushed the door slowly open. I was so scared I almost peed in my pants. Now how would that look? A superhero that needs training pants. I bet that never happens in the comic books.

When the bad guy stepped into the room, I stood up, put my fists on my hips and pushed out my chest as far as I could in what I thought was a really good superhero pose. The bad guy started laughing as soon as he got a look at me.

"Kid, what are you doing in there? Who do you think you are some kinda superhero? I didn't know they made tights that small." He chuckled.

"They're NOT tights! And I am a superhero. I'm The Supadupa Kid!" I said in a voice so deep I almost hurt myself. He laughed even harder, then grabbed my arm and pulled me out of the closet.

"Hey, let go of me!" I shouted. *Run, Javon, run!* I heard Ronald shouting in my ear. I thought about running, but heroes don't run, heroes fight!

"If you surrender now, I won't hurt you," I told him as I yanked my arm from his grasp.

"You hurt me? Kid, you couldn't even hurt my feelings." he grunted.

Javon, blast him. Think of something happy! Ronald shouted in my ear.

"I can't. I'm too mad!"

"Who are you talking to kid?" The robber asked puzzled. I could feel the anger building up inside me, and was surprised when my fingertips began to crackle with electricity. Ronald was still screaming into my ear, but my attention was focused on the goon in front of me. I clapped my hands together and rubbed them back and forth to try to build up as much friction as I could. I could feel the energy getting stronger and stronger. The goon suddenly stopped laughing when he saw the glowing ball of electricity that was forming between my palms.

I smiled when I saw the look of fear on his face as I created a perfectly round, glowing sphere the size of a baseball that was crackling loudly on my palm.

"Ka-Boom, Sucka!" I shouted and pitched the lightning ball right into his chest. It knocked him off his feet and he crashed into the wall with a big *THUD*. He was knocked out cold but my fingertips were still sparkling, and Ronald was still screaming in my ear.

"Take it easy, brain boy, calm down. I'm fine, but you're not going to believe what I just did to bad guy number one! This is the coolest thing ever. I knocked that sucka out!"

"Whoa!" Ronald said, breathing heavily.

"Whoa is right! This is awesome, but I've got to calm down. It isn't over yet, and I'm getting waaaay too excited." I looked down at the gun he'd been carrying and noticed that it looked kind of strange. I picked it up and shook it. There was some kind of liquid in it. Although it looked like a real gun it wasn't. It was a water gun. The robbers were sticking up the bank with water guns? These have to be the dumbest bad guys ever and it's time for them to go down. I confidently flew down the stairs to the first floor where the hostages were being held. They were at the far end of the room but I could see them all, the hostages and the bad guys. They were carrying water guns too. Now that I'm sure I wouldn't be getting any holes in Ronald's expensive super-suit, I knew it was hero time! I swooped into the center of the room and landed in my hero pose. Everyone gasped with surprise.

"I'm the Supadupa Kid. Put down your (*chuckle*) weapons and you won't get hurt," I shouted.

Two of the bad guys ran to tackle me and **BOOM**. Bad guy number two took a lightning bolt to the chest and **BOOM** I shot a light fixture off the ceiling that hit bad guy number three in the head, and he folded like a lawn chair. Only one bad guy left. Everybody was looking at me with their mouths wide open, including bad guy number four, the leader. My hands sparkled with energy at my sides.

"Are you going to surrender or do you want the shock of your life?" *Now that's a cool catch phrase! I heard Ronald say.*

"If you take one more step towards me, kid, you're gonna get it!"

"What am I gonna get, a shower? Okay, chump, you asked for it." **KA-BOOM!** I hit him with a lightning bolt so hard it knocked him through the front door. He rolled down the stairs and landed right in front of Officer Taylor. All was silent for a moment before the crowd erupted into cheers.

The hostages ran to me, thanking me, hugging me; one lady even pinched my cheeks. I pushed my way through the crowd just as the police swarmed into the building.

"STOP!" one of the officers yelled at me.

"I don't think so," I said over my shoulder and flew back up the stairs and out the utility closet window. As I zipped over the building I could see flashes from dozens of cameras below.

In a few minutes, I was back in Ronald's bedroom. I changed into my regular clothes, finish my homework and rushed to get home before dinner. At the table all my family could talk about was the attempted robbery at the Dollar Bill Bank that they had seen on the news.

"I can't believe a kid in orange tights saved the bank from being robbed?" Dad said.

"They weren't tights," I mumbled under my breath.

"And it is very refreshing that he didn't stick around to take all the credit," Mom said.

"There's no way a kid in a *super-suit* could stop a bank robbery. That's ridiculous. Please pass the peas," I said and somehow managed to keep a straight face.

13

The next morning when Denise and I hopped on the bus to school everyone was talking about the kid that captured the bank robbers. Some kids saw him on the news, some kids read about him in the newspaper but everybody, even the school bus driver, was talking about him. He could fly, one kid said. He can shoot lightning bolts from his hands, said another. I even heard someone shout that the mysterious kid superhero could lift skyscrapers and throw them at the moon. Man, these kids were eating this stuff up. Denise sat down with her friends while I spotted an empty seat next to Erika.

"Is anyone sitting here?" I asked nervously.

"Nope. Have a seat, she said with a smile. "So what do you think about all this superhero talk?" She asked.

"I don't buy it. All the pictures of that kid are blurry; it looks like a giant orange colored turkey flying through the air." She giggled and I relaxed a little.

"What about the hostages? They saw him, didn't they?" Erika asked.

"Those people were scared out of their minds, who knows what they saw." I replied. "If someone saved my life, I'd probably think they were a superhero too. Those poor people had no idea that all they were in danger of was getting their underwear soggy from the water guns those robbers were carrying."

"They had water guns? It didn't say that in the paper." Erika said curiously.

"Yeah...um...I think I heard that on the news this morning. Anyway, they were stressed out, they could have seen anything."

"Yeah, I guess that's true. When I get stressed out, I see the weirdest things too. Once after an argument with my older brother, I was looking out the window, and I thought I saw a guy fly up and rescue a cat stuck in a tree."

"Wow, that is kinda nuts," I said awkwardly and changed the subject.

When we got to the auditorium it was Supadupa pandemonium. Big kids, little kids, the principal, everybody was talking about him. Ronald pulled me to the side and whispered, "Can you believe this?"

"This is crazy. I think the Supadupa Kid needs to stay out of the spotlight for a little while."

Just then Hoody bumped me hard from behind.

"I know that was you at the bank yesterday. Who do you think you are? You're no hero, you're a zero."

"Look, Hoody, I don't want any trouble."

"Well that's too bad. You could never take me out as easily as you did those bank robbers. I'm stronger than you. Why don't you meet me after school behind the bleachers, and I'll show you who's stronger."

"I told you, Hoody, I don't want any trouble."

"I knew it; you're nothing but a coward, you and your little playmate, Donald."

"Excuse me, but my name is Ronald, not Donald," Ronald stated. Hoody looked around, making sure no one was looking. He lowered his sunglasses revealing his ruby red eyes and gave Ronald another ZAP to the chest. "Ouch!" Ronald screamed as he clutched his chest in pain.

"I don't care if your name is Ronald McDonald. The next time my glasses come down, I will be aiming at you," he said and poked me in the chest.

"Ronald, are you okay?" I was mad, real mad. This was the second time Hoody hurt my friend. There wouldn't be a third time!

"Yeah I'm okay, but aren't the superhero and the villain supposed to exchange blows? Usually the sidekick doesn't get hurt in the comics. This stinks! I'm going to have to wear an aluminum foil shirt to reflect Hoody's rays."

"My best friend isn't coming to school looking like wrapped up leftovers. I'll deal with Hoody and you stop sounding like a baby when you get zapped."

"Sure, make fun of me now but you'll be apologizing when Hoody finally zaps you."

14

The rest of the day was cool. We had our final classes at the high school. All the Supadupa chatter had died down, and I didn't see Hoody again. I couldn't wait to go home. When the end of the school day came I was so happy I could feel myself starting to float. If I did that in front of my classmates my life would be over. I leaned against a tree and waited for Denise, wishing I could fly home instead of taking the bus. My heart skipped a beat when I saw Erika walking towards me.

"Hey, Javon.

"Hey Erica."

"I'm so glad its Friday. What are you doing this weekend?"

I wanted to say, *Oh, fighting crime, rescuing innocent people, you know the usual.* But instead I said, "Nothing, just hanging out with Ronald."

"Well..umm..I'm going to see the new movie, *Alienman3,* wanna come?"

"HECK YES! Errr...I mean sure, that would be great," I said. I was so excited, I had to grab onto the tree to keep from floating off the ground.

"Cool. I'll come by tomorrow around twelve o'clock."

"Great, see you then."

That night at the dinner table Dad, Mom, and Denise were still talking about the Supadupa Kid.

"Everyone is going crazy trying to figure out who this kid is. Is he an alien? Is he the result of a government experiment? Nobody knows," Dad sighed.

"I hope that he doesn't get famous and go on some crazy reality show." Mom stated.

"I think the Supadupa Kid needs to go to the gym because he doesn't have any muscles and I hate his tights," Denise chortled.

"They're NOT tights." I snapped but then decided if you can't beat em, join em. I became the biggest Supadupa cheerleader.

"I think his costume is way cool and man, does he seem smart, and did you know he can fly faster than a speeding bullet. I even heard he can throw skyscrapers to the moon!"

"Okay guys, that's enough supadupa talk for one day. How was school today?" Mom asked.

"School was fine but I was wondering if I could go to the movies tomorrow?"

"To see what and with whom?" Dad asked.

"*Alienman3* with Erika Harris. I'll use my allowance money."

"Oooh, Erika-n-Javon sitting in a tree, K-I-S-S-I-N-G, first comes love, then comes marriage, then comes...."

"Alright, Denise, that's enough. No singing at the dinner table."

"That's fine, Javon, you may go out with Erika. I know Mr. and Dr. Harris very well, and Erika is a very nice young lady. Just make sure you're home in time for dinner."

"Yes Mom, no problem."

15

At eleven forty-five a.m., on Saturday morning, I was outside waiting for Erika. I have to admit, I was a little nervous. I'd never gone to the movies with a girl before. I made sure not to wear any metal. No belts or jewelry, nothing that would make me lose my grip on gravity. When Erika and her dad pulled up I noticed how new and clean the car looked.

"Hello, Erika, hello, Mr. Harris. Nice car!"

"Thanks, Javon, I just picked it up yesterday, and I must admit this car cost a pretty penny. It's got more gadgets than a rocket ship. Take for instance..."

"DAD!" Erika said, frustrated.

"Sorry, honey, I get a little carried away. I love this car. So, Javon, how have you been feeling since the incident? My wife made me promise I'd ask."

"Tell Dr. Harris, I'm shockingly well and thanks for asking." I chuckled.

Before we went into the theater, Erika asked her father to pick us up at three o'clock at Al's Ice Cream Parlor next door.

At the concession stand we got a large bucket of popcorn with extra butter and two drinks. We sat in the last row of the theater in the center aisle. The movie was great. There was lots of action and drama, which got me pretty excited. Erika and I had our hands in the popcorn bucket at the same time when there was a big explosion on screen. It scared me just as our fingers touched, and I accidently gave her a little shock.

"Ouch!" she yelped. "What in the world was that?

"I must be full of static electricity from the carpet, sorry about that!" I said.

"Wow! That was some shock. I'm glad I'm not wearing a wool sweater, or I might have blown up."

After the movie we went to the ice cream parlor and sat right near the window so we could watch out for her dad. We talked about how great the movie was and that we knew there would be an *Alienman4*, and 5, and 27. Then we talked about school and which teacher was the coolest, which student was the dorkiest (Ronald won hands down), and stuff like that. Things were going great when suddenly I felt uneasy, like we were being watched. I looked around the ice cream shop, but the only thing that looked weird was Al, the owner, who was juggling donut holes. But I couldn't shake the feeling that something was wrong. I looked up and down. I looked at every car and passerby until I finally saw him. Hoody was standing on the corner. He stood there just watching us with his arms crossed. When he noticed me, he smirked, waved, and then he put one hand on the metal post that was connected to the traffic light. With his other hand he pulled down his sunglasses. His eyes turned bright red and then the traffic lights turned green, IN ALL FOUR DIRECTIONS! It only took seconds before I heard the screeching of tires and a glass shattering *CRASH!* There was complete chaos on the road. Cars were mangled and people were yelling. Hoody waved to me and casually walked away. I threw some money down on the table, grabbed Erika's hand and ran outside, surprised to find no one was badly injured.

"Oh no!" Erika said when she noticed that one of the cars in the pile-up was her dad's.

"NOT MY NEW CAR, NOT MY NEW CAR!" he screamed. The car was totaled, but at least he wasn't hurt. I looked around for Hoody, but he was nowhere to be found. Hoody's powers were getting the best of him, he was losing control. He was getting way too dangerous and he had to be stopped before someone got seriously hurt or worse. I knew I was the only one who could stop him.

Mr. Harris had to wait for the police to arrive so he paid for a taxi to take us home.

"That was so crazy. There were cars piled up everywhere. What could have caused the accident?" Erika asked as we drove away.

"I don't know, the traffic signal freaked out somehow," I said, half truthfully.

"You had a funny look on your face just before the accident. Did you see anything strange?"

"No, of course not," I responded. I wanted to tell her I saw Hoody use his powers to make all the traffic lights turn green but telling her the Easter bunny caused the accidents was probably more believable.

The taxi dropped me off first so I made Erika promise to give me a call when she got home. As the cab drove away, I had the feeling again that I was being watched. I looked around but the only person I could see was Denise, with her big head sticking out the window, yelling, "Did you kiss her? Javon kissed Erika!"

16

I called Ronald as soon as I got in the house and told him what happened. He couldn't believe it.

"Hoody's gone pecans," Ronald stated.

"Pecans, what does that mean?" I asked.

"You know, pecans, pistachios, cashews...NUTS!" Ronald said.

"Ronald, you are the Mayor of Dorkville," I said shaking my head. "Now focus, we have to figure out a way to stop Hoody."

"Wait a minute, the computers flashing." Ronald interrupted. "There's an emergency about a disturbance at Crazyworld." Ronald said as he read the alert that flashed across the screen.

"Crazyworld, the old amusement park, isn't it about to be torn down? What in the world could be going on over there?" I wondered.

"It says something about rides running by themselves and beams of red light coming from the area." Ronald read the monitor. "Wait a minute, there's also a report of a taxi cab right down the street from your house that got struck by lightning."

"Lightening? There isn't a cloud in the sky." I said.

"Uh oh, it says there was a girl in the cab too and now she's missing.

"It's gotta be Hoody! And I bet he took Erika." I said.

"And I bet it's a trap." Ronald said nervously.

"Okay, that's it! Shocking you with lightning bolts and making you cry like a baby is one thing, but kidnapping my girl is another."

"Hey, I did not cry like a baby, and did you just call Erika your girl?" exclaimed Ronald.

"Uh, that's not what I meant, I mean, um. That's not important right now, Erika, I mean Ronald! We have to focus. She could be in real danger."

"Yes, I know, and I've got an idea that just might stop Hoody," Ronald said.

"Great! I'm going to change into the Supadupa Kid, rescue Erika, and take down Hoody. But first, I've got to call my Mom."

"Call your Mom? You know, most superheroes don't usually need permission from their Mom to save damsels in distress," teased Ronald.

"I'm calling to let her know her little boy will be home late for dinner.

What do you want from me? I'm a Momma's boy."

17

(Meanwhile at the House of Mirrors in Crazyworld)

"Hoody, why are you doing this, let me go!" demanded Erika.

"I'm going to prove that the Supadupa Kid is a Supadupa wimp. And since he's your friend, it's only a matter of time before he comes for you, and when he does, I will crush him."

"The Supadupa Kid is not my friend. I've never even met him before," protested Erika.

"I saw you two having ice cream together earlier today," sneered Hoody.

"The only person I had ice cream with today is Javon. OH MY GOODNESS! Javon is the Supadupa Kid? That explains the shock. Cool, I went on a date with a superhero, and now his archenemy has kidnapped me. This is so awesome. I will be the envy of all the girls in school."

"Hey, this isn't cool, this isn't awesome. You're in real serious danger," Hoody said adamantly.

"Sure, sure Hoody. Just let me go before I break a nail."

"Erika, I don't think you're taking me seriously. Let's see if this changes your mind."

Hoody pulled down his sunglasses and aimed at a pile of boxes in the corner. **ZAP!** In a flash the boxes caught on fire. Smoke quickly filled the room.

"Hoody, please put it out. I'm sorry," Erika coughed. Hoody yanked a fire extinguisher from the wall and used it to put out the flames.

"When Javon gets here, I hope he kicks your butt," Erika snapped.

"Impossible. My powers are stronger than his, and as soon as that punk gets here I'll prove it."

18

From up above, my town looks like a giant birthday cake with millions of candles waiting to be blown out. Flying over it in any other situation would be the most awesome thing in the world but tonight I had other things on my mind. I had to stop Hoody once and for all.

As I was rocketing towards Crazyworld, I could see smoke coming from one of the buildings.

That's it, that must be where Hoody is. I know he is expecting me, so I must be careful. Who knows what kind of trap he has waiting for me.

I landed on the roof of the building because I figured he would expect me to come through the front or back door. I blasted a hole in the roof big enough for me to get through. I flew down and landed in a room filled with mirrors.

"Oh great, I'm in the House of Mirrors. If I break one of these I'll have seven years of bad luck," I whispered.

"You have bad luck now, Supadopey. I'm so glad you could

join us," Hoody laughed sinisterly from somewhere in the room.

Where was he? I could hear him, but I couldn't see him. No matter where I turned I could only see reflections of myself. Then, out of nowhere, **ZAP!** A lightning bolt hit me in the chest. It was so powerful that it threw me across the room, slamming me into one of the mirrors, shattering it into pieces. "*OWWWWW!*" I screamed. Boy, that hurt. It felt like I got punched by a gorilla. Ronald was right, that *HURT!* I'll never call him a baby again. Now, I definitely have seven years of bad luck! I stumbled to my feet and a second later... **ZAP**! I flew into another mirror, shattering this one into pieces, too. ***ARRRG!*** Those lightning bolts were no joke. I wasn't sure if I could stand another shot when I finally saw him. From my knees, I balled my hands into angry fists, building up the energy inside them and with a neon burst I let it fly! A blue bolt of lightning shot from my fingers and hit him in the stomach. I gave him all I had but all he did was laugh.

"Is that the best you've got? All you did was tickle my tummy. You're no match for me," he growled.

Then he pulled down his sunglasses and hit me with a red bolt of energy that knocked me out cold!

I woke up in a dark room tied to a post and I wasn't alone.

"Javon, Javon, wake up."

"Erika?"

"Yes, it's me. Are you okay?"

"No I'm not. My chest hurts, I've got a headache and I'm tied to a post in a dark room with you. Wait a minute...maybe I am okay. How about you? You okay?

"Yeah, I'm fine and by the way, I love your tights."

"They're not tights!! It's all one piece, it's my Supadupa suit! Oh no, you know who I am, don't you?"

"Hoody told me, but your secret is safe with me. I promise not to tell anyone—if we make it out of here."

"Don't worry, we're getting out of here right now."

I closed my eyes and concentrated on good things, and my strength slowly came back. I zapped the rope and it turned to dust, but before we could escape Hoody burst through the door.

"Hey chump!" Hoody yelled. "Where do you think you're going?"

Zap! I ducked and a red lightning bolt flew over my head.

"Hey, no aiming for the head! This haircut cost my Pops fifteen bucks."

"I would have zapped your whole head off for free!"

I clapped and hit him with another jolt that knocked him on his butt. He fired back with a sizzler that bounced off the wall and hit Erika, knocking her unconscious.

I blasted a hole through the wall and was happy to see the moon lighting up the park. I took off running.

"Come back and fight, you coward," roared Hoody. A bolt of energy shot past my ear and blasted a horse right off the Merry-Go-Round. I ducked and dodged and bobbed until I saw the food court. It was just ahead, and there was the area I was looking for—the cotton candy stand. I skidded to a stop and turned around, facing Hoody.

"Okay Hoody, enough is enough, you're going down!"

"BRING IT, PUNK!"

BOOM! A red bolt shot from his eyes. *BOOM!* I shot a blue bolt back at him. *ZAP, BOOM, CRACKLE!* We were shooting lightning bolts like cowboys in a Western showdown. The sky was filled with so much red and blue it looked like a fireworks display. Then **BAM**! I took a big bolt to the chest. I flew backwards over the cotton candy counter and crash landed into a pile of boxes. I looked up to find Hoody standing on the counter glaring down at me. His eyes were bright red and ready to give me the biggest shock ever.

"This is the end for you—any last words, Supadopey?"

"Yeah. I hope you like cotton candy. **KA-BOOM SUCKA!**" I clapped my hands together and released a stream of blue energy so strong it hit him in the chest and blasted him into the air. He flew across the room and smashed through the top of the cotton candy machine. He landed in the machine so hard the walls shook, knocking over pounds of pink sugar that spilled into the machine.

I flew to the cotton candy machine, flipped the switch and gave it a jolt to power it up. The machine started spinning Hoody around. I jolted it a little more and it picked up speed. It moved faster and faster making cotton candy that wrapped Hoody up tightly. "Get me outta here," Hoody screamed. He looked really dizzy and even turned a little green from spinning so fast. I thought he was going to barf. In a matter of seconds, the machine had wrapped Hoody in a pink cocoon of cotton candy, and then I pulled the Supadupa Glue Ronald gave me out of my belt and squeezed the entire tube into the machine. When the glue hardened, Hoody looked like a pink cotton candy statue, but I could still hear him yelling, "Get me outta here, I'm afraid of the dark!" With one big blast I zapped the metal inside the machine. "*ARRRRRG*!" Hoody yelled before he was finally quiet.

It was over. Hoody was defeated and I had Ronald to thank for it! I used the same idea Ronald used when he won the state science fair. He used a Styrofoam cup to contain electricity. Instead of a Styrofoam cup, I used cotton candy. The metal inside the machine acted like a conductor, transferring the electricity from Hoody's body into the cotton candy. Ronald may be a dork, but he's a smart dork. Looks like I owe brain boy big time.

"Hey, Hoody, maybe you can eat your way out!" I yelled. I could hear him mumble something about my mom.

In the distance I heard police sirens coming closer. Man, it's about time the cops showed up. They should have been here a long time ago. There must have been a special on doughnuts at Al's again.

I flew back to the House of Mirrors to check on Erika. She was just waking up when I walked in.

"Are you alright?" I asked as I helped her up.

"My head is killing me and what's with the crazy costume? Where am I?" she asked as she rubbed her head.

"You're at Crazyworld amusement park and....wait a minute—you don't know who I am?"

"Huh, no, I don't think so. Are those tights you're wearing?" she asked.

"They're not...sigh..yeah, they're tights, you like them?"

"Cute." She said as we walked out of the House of Mirrors and saw a team of officers running towards us led by Officer Taylor.

"Hello, Officer. This young lady needs to be taken home and she could probably use an icepack, too. Also, in the old food court you'll find a big pink statue of cotton candy, but I wouldn't try to eat it. There's is a kid in there that kidnapped the girl. You might want to ask him about the fire at Booker T. Washington Elementary and Middle School." I said as I started to fly away.

"Hey, kid, you're not going anywhere. We've got a lot of

questions for you," said Officer Taylor.

"Sorry, Officer, but if I don't get home before dinner, I'm going to get supadupa grounded. Later!"

SWOOSH! I took to the sky, waving goodbye to the officers and Erika. While in the air I contacted Ronald and told him the whole story. This had been some weekend.

19

Things slowly returned to normal in the neighborhood. School re-opened and it was cool to be back in our regular classrooms instead of the cafeteria or auditorium.

Ronald and I decided that SDK needed to lay low for a little while. So my super-suit has been hidden in the back of his closet for a few weeks. I don't miss it too much because it is a little itchy and with the media going crazy trying to discover my secret identity, it's smart to lay low for a while.

One of the best stories I heard on the news was that the Supadupa Kid was really a robot created by a mad scientist hidden away on a deserted island somewhere in the Caribbean. Hey, that works for me.

Unfortunately, the great date Erika and I had when we went to the movies meant nothing because she couldn't remember it. When Hoody's lightning bolt knocked her out, she lost a whole week of her memory. She didn't remember the Supadupa Kid, being kidnapped, or even going to the movies with me. Whenever she sees me she just says hello and doesn't give me a second thought. All of those laser beams to the chest were for nothing and I'm not even sure if I'll ever grow hair there. I finally got the courage up to ask her to go to the movies with me to see *Alienman3* but she blew me off with some lame excuse about having to wash her hamster. I wanted to remind her that she once asked *me* out to the movies, but I don't think she would have believed me. I even thought about zapping her with another bolt of electricity so maybe she would remember, but Ronald talked me out of it.

Thankfully the battle at Crazyworld removed Hoody's powers

for good. I'll never look at cotton candy the same way again. Sure, cotton candy can be bad on the teeth but it's even badder on bad guys!

When everyone found out that Hoody was behind the fires, and the disturbance at Crazyworld, his mom and dad decided that they all needed to get out of town, so they moved to Mississippi. Rumor has it that instead of being sent to Stoney Rock Juvenile Detention Center for Boys, he had to scrape the gum off the bottom of every desk in every school in his new hometown with his teeth. GROSS! If that's true, his choppers are probably as dirty as his hooded sweatshirt now. I can't figure out why he never told anyone that I'm the Supadupa Kid. Maybe he figured with all the bad things he did, no one would believe him anyway.

Ronald and I are closer than ever. We hang out almost every day after school. We usually go to his house and do homework until it's time for me to go home for dinner. We used to play video games until I got too excited and blew up the console. Sometimes we listen to 911 calls just to see what's going on in the city, but I have to admit, it makes me miss that itchy suit.

Today when an emergency call came in it was too tempting to ignore.

'...base to unit 2451. We have reports of a cat stuck in a tree at 105 Linden Street. Please report to the location immediately...'

"Isn't that the same place where you fried that little girl's cat crispy?" Ronald asked with his eyes wide.

"Yeah, I think it is." We both turned toward the closet as if we could hear the Supadupa suit calling us. I looked at Ronald and he looked back anxiously.

"Go on, go save that kitty!"

He didn't have to tell me twice, I jumped into the closet and came out with my super-suit on. In three steps I was across the room and out the window. In a few minutes I could see the little girl with the red hair standing right under the exact same tree calling for her cat to come down. The cat was perched comfortably, licking his paws and ignoring the little girl. When the cat saw me flying in, it stood on all fours and hissed at me and then scurried down the tree into the arms of the little girl. I landed gracefully by her side and smiled.

"I guess Fluffy still hasn't forgiven me, huh?" I asked and the little girl shook her head. The cat hissed at me again, and I took that as my cue to get lost. I floated slowly into the air and waved goodbye.

"HEY SUPADUPA KID, I'M EATING ALL MY VEGETABLES!" she shouted as I took off into the sky. I gave her a thumb's up, winked, and flew away in search of another way to save the city from peril.

THE END

.....for now!

AUTHOR / ILLUSTRATOR

Real Name: Tyrone Allan Jackson
Alias: Fly Ty
Occupation: Author Extraordinaire
Origin: Bronx, NY
D.O.B. July 31
Current Headquarters: Big Head Books Secret Compound - Location unknown
Superpowers: Superb attitude, supersonic smile, towering ambition
Weaknesses: Chocolate Chip Cookies, soul food and cold weather
Arch Enemies: Slacker Dude, Idontlike2read MAN and anyone who takes my cookies
Mission: To bestow upon every child in the world the power of reading

Real Name: Jonathan David Shears
Alias: The Red Beast
Occupation: Master Designer
Origin: Adams, MA
D.O.B. September 13
Current Headquarters: Parts Unknown
Superpowers: Hyper-realistic illusions, dimensional distortion, titanic tenacity
Weaknesses: Action figures, commercials for homeless pets, and "The Sleeper"
Arch Enemies: Mr. Digital World, Carbo-Hydrate, and the words "I CAN'T"
Mission: To protect the realm of imagination

ACKNOWLEDGEMENTS

Thank you to my Big Head Books family
Martique Jackson, Nicole Davies, Eddie Taylor
and Donna Todd Rivers.

Special thanks to the following:
Diane Jamison, LaVaughn Davies, James
Jackson, Bruce Dean, Manzo Jackson,
Jasmine Jamison, Jermaine Foster, Judy
Williamson, Theresa Williams, Earl, Evelyn
and Frankie Taylor, The Fleming Family, The
Frederick Family, The Taylor Family, The
Dews Family, Eric Milton, Denise Mediavilla,
Jimmy Hall, Carver Bank, Berkshire Bank,
Greylock Federal Credit Union, Minisink
Community Center and Club Read Deal, New
York Mission Society, Children of Promise,
Children's Village, Litworld, Susan Herriot and
Cool Boys Read, The Hue-Man Bookstore
and the Cornellier family.

Big shout out to Jon Shears, the most talented
illustrator on the planet and one awesome
dude!

You are all SUPADUPA!

For more information about The Supadupa Kid and other Big Head Books, check out our website www.bigheadbooks.com or find us on Facebook or Twitter by searching The Supadupa Kid or Big Head Books.

.....gEt bOoKiN